This book belongs to

Hillyfield Academy
Higham Hill Road
London
E17 6ED

_____

_____

Other books by the author

The Idiot Family at Home

The Idiot Family on Holiday *to be published in 2013*

Perfectly Splendid Stories Collection

Archie Dingletrotter's Flying Caravan

Desmond's Dragon *to be published in 2013*

Perfectly Silly Stories Collection

Petronella Pumperknickel-Pinkstocking-Berck and Big Wart

The Phantom Sock-Snatcher *to be published in 2013*

Petronella Pumpernickel-Pinkstocking-Berck and Big Wart

written by A J Stairmand

From the Perfectly Silly Stories Collection

Published by Stairmand Publishing 2012
Copyright © A J Stairmand 2012

Illustrations: James Stairmand

A CIP catalogue record for this book is available from the British Library.

ISBN 978-0-9569234-8-6

Layout design by: Designsweet. www.designsweet.co.uk

Printed by: Lavenham Press Limited
Arbons House, 47 Water Street, Lavenham CO10 9RN

Distributed by: York Publishing Services
64 Hallfield Road, Layerthorpe, York YO31 7ZQ

Acknowledgements

There are many people I would like to thank for all the support and help whilst writing and publishing this book. First of all, I would like to thank my ever-patient and truly wonderful editors Sharon Burns, Kathy Norris and Michael, (my husband and biggest critic). Also, my sons James and Will, and my father, all of whom have been unwavering in their help, advice and expertise and, of course, their positive attitude.

In particular, I have to thank Kathy for her expertise, tireless commitment to the design of the layout, the finer details of the book, and the countless conversations over every single aspect.

I also have to give an enormous thank you to James Banfield, for his support and advice which has been invaluable, throughout the publication of this book. Adding to this, I have to thank Leigh Hemmings for her time, ideas and enthusiasm for promoting my work this year, and always making me laugh!

I must thank my son James for his quirky, and truly sharp illustrations of the characters and situations in the book. His vision and ideas have really brought the book to life. Also, I have to thank him for all his time and care working tirelessly on my website, it is very much appreciated.

In fact, as I write this, I wish to thank Virginia Loveridge at Waterstones Chelmsford, and Dean Miguel at Waterstones Croydon, for unwavering support this year. Their enthusiasm and belief has been inspirational and so appreciated.

Most importantly, it's you the reader I wish to thank for reading my book. I really hope that you like it, enjoy it and have fun with the names and characters.

Chapter 1

By the time she was in Year Eight Petronella Pumpernickel-Pinkstocking-Berck had sort of **'kissed'** every weak, wimpy boy in the lower school.

Actually, that's not quite true, as in most cases, being a bit of a bruiser of a girl, she'd twisted their arms with a backstabbing Chinese burn and threatened to take their lunch money. Since she had the muscles of an all-in wrestler, nobody was going to put up a fight.  **To make matters worse**, her mother bellowed to her every morning that, if she continued to kiss boys – especially those who didn't wash or had bad breath – something **horrible would happen to her mouth.** And, can I tell you that, Ma Metronella

Pumpernickel-Pinkingstocking-Berck was not a woman to argue with. Her muscles were even bigger; they were in fact

huge

a bit like stand-up saucepans, shovelled underneath the skin in her arms. The sort that made men go weak with fear or admiration, depending how well you got on with her.

Petronella never listened to her mother; what would she know about boys and kissing? She was far too old to understand these things, as she had never been young, or had even gone to school. So, Petronella thought her mother was silly and, *she* read the weekend papers (ugh!!).

Chapter 2

At school, Petronella spent most of her time in lessons deciding who her next victim would be, and often, when others were writing, she was defining her list, working out the next point of action.

Since her muscles, for a Year Eight, were like almond-shaped balloons

stuffed underneath her shirt, every time she wrote her desk shuddered, so did the chair. This meant her teachers knew 'exactly' when she was working. Well, that's what they thought, at least until they questioned her, or asked her to read out in class. Nobody dared to whisper, as when she spoke in a booming voice, it reverberated generally down the corridor, overpowering the most intense lessons in its wake. So you can imagine what it was like when she was

upset or
angry or, even worse,
excited;

her voice had a crescendo like a volcano
rumbling throughout the day.

She was the best person to
have in tug-of-war and
often played
f o o t b a l l ,
commanding
all the positions
from goal to
centre-half. Yes, she
was certainly something else; different from
the rest of the girls who loved fashion,
nail-varnish, skinny jeans and majorettes.

Not for her,
the twirling, pink, frilly, petticoats
and little white boots with
silver-petal laces; nor the
ringlet-sponged hair with

glitter and sequins, surrounding a pointed, pink hat perfectly stapled in with hair grips.

Not for her,

the white gloves which wafted, weaved and wobbled with dancing canes to beguiled audiences everywhere.

No!

Petronella Pumpernickel-Pinkstocking-Berck had hobbies of her own, making tractors and farm machinery, then selling them on eBay for a small profit.

Now, you might wonder how a once sweet and bright child would end up being a mechanic's best mate at weekends, when she could be out in town buying stuff for a school disco. Petronella didn't need discos, as she could take or leave boys – after she'd 'kissed' them of course!

Chapter 3

The Pumpernickel-Pinkstocking-Berck house was slightly different from any other. It was built near a scrap-yard on the edge of town, close to the rubbish tip; so it was a perfect environment to practise the skills needed for her hobby, building tractors, which was unusual, and challenging.

The house was made out of

spare scraps of steel,

concrete and

metal objects,

which had been soldered together by her parents since she was a baby.

By the time she was five, the building, rather than a house, had grown to six stories and had a multitude of leftover materials welded to form its shape and design. It was quite industrial from the outside, and older members of the community whispered to each other quietly, that it looked like part of a steel plant.

However, the family was always told otherwise, so that Pa Pumpernickel-Pinkstocking-Berck wouldn't get out his shotgun at those making fun of his individually designed kingdom.

Such were her skills and talents, that Petronella could take apart a tractor, in the same way one would unpick the seam of a piece of clothing. She had the county record for building her own steamroller, (small) quicker than any farmer in the area. Yes, she was a force to be reckoned with, in and out of school.

But it was the kissing lark that caused the most consternation amongst everyone.

In truth, although she'd set her heart on beating any school record for kissing, **sixty percent (60%)** of her victims (none of whom had brushed their teeth), just took the second option and gave her their lunch money. **Twenty percent (20%)** did it for a bet and won bucket-loads in the playground.

Sadly, the other

twenty percent (20%)

hadn't the strength

to avoid her.

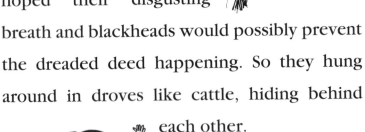

Of course, the boys hoped their disgusting breath and blackheads would possibly prevent the dreaded deed happening. So they hung around in droves like cattle, hiding behind each other.

But, one by one, they had to deal with the dreadful consequences of the **"Pumpernickel Holdfast"**, as it was called.

24

By the end of the Easter Term, Petronella began her holiday in the safe knowledge that she had, despite not having a skinny waist; despite not being a majorette; despite not wearing nail-varnish, she had done a "holdfast" on every boy in the lower school – and, in some cases, got incredibly rich at the same time.

Chapter 4

It all changed in the summer term, when there was a new boy in town and he started school. Known as **Big Wart,** he was built like a small Amazon river, with a chest that spanned the width of the corridor, and muscles that had to be carried by minions.

His arms were so big and hairy that he

proudly combed his wrists in class - with a yellow comb with the inscription "Big Bad Wart".

His hair was a halo of blonde curls which he kept under a rugby band and England cap. When he was asked to remove it, he'd tower over the teachers, fold his arms, smile and walk on.

Nobody crossed Big Wart, who

indeed was just like his name, full of warts and blackheads from too much greasy food and fizzy drinks.

So it came to pass, on the first day, Big Wart had some lessons with Petronella - History, English and P.E. - and she was shocked to

see how he picked people to sit next to:
every girl - but not her.

Didn't **he** know who *she* was?

All the girls smiled at him, and he smiled back; they dropped their pens, and he picked them up; he'd say something, and they would all laugh. She looked on while this happened. For once, Petronella Pumpernickel -Pinkstocking-Berck wasn't the centre of attention, and she didn't like it!

Flexing her balloon-like muscles, she lifted up

the teacher's table with her thumb. Whilst every other wimp in the class gasped, cheered and bowed, Big Wart got out his speedway magazine and tried to do the quiz on the last

page. Unable to contain her shock, Petronella crushed the table in two with her mighty earth-shattering muscles; Big Wart picked his nose.

Still, unable to comprehend his lack of attention and indifference, she got a row of tables, stood them on top of each other, balanced them on her mighty arm and tried to tap dance at the same time.

Bored, Big Wart stuck the plugs into his ears and listened to his iPod collection.

At this point, the girls goggled in awe, as they were just honoured to see such strength from another female; the boys shuddered and hoped and prayed they weren't on her list for the day.

So, whilst the rest of the class treated her like a wrestling goddess, Big Wart only responded to 'Girls Like Them'; small, straight hair, pretty, feminine, who laughed and smiled.

He didn't respond to Petronella's gesture to build a tractor in her scrap yard after school, or the offer of taking a mini steam-roller to pieces; he was going to watch the girls in his class practise their dances for the majorette tournaments!

Then something terrible happened to her mouth and teeth...

Chapter 5

Smiling and smirking at the back of the classroom, was a boy who had never forgiven Petronella for getting him in a "Pumpernickel-Holdfast". Mercury Bitterack was determined to get his revenge, by secretly casting a spell on her to make Petronella look foolish. Staring at Big Wart, Mercury Bitterack realised this was his chance to humiliate Petronella.

Petronella screamed and cried out loud!

It couldn't get any worse. Then, just as her mother had predicted, something awful happened to her!

Her teeth fell out and

suddenly tufts of grass, which would need cutting everyday, began to replace them.

At the back of the classroom Mercury Bitterack sniggered to himself.

He had kept it a secret from everybody – even his parents – that he could cast spells. Secretly, he had dabbled in magic since he was a young child, and had been successful when casting spells on others throughout his strange childhood. For example, once, when his parents had wanted him to go to bed, rather than cry and throw his bears out of his cot, he screamed a spell, which made it light twenty-four hours a day.

His sad parents, unaware of their naughty son's antics, just hired people to play with him whilst they tried to sleep. Another time, when he hadn't got all his spellings right and the teacher had told him off, he cast a spell giving her horse's hooves and a tail.

Since nobody had a clue that it was Mercury causing all this terrible commotion and trouble, his life was perfect.

However, there was one drawback: he could **only cast five spells a year**, which was probably wise as he might be doing it all the time.

Never forgetting how upset he felt, Mercury Bitterack was determined to find the perfect spell that would make her look foolish in front of the whole school.

Even though she was big, strong and tough, he also knew she was vain: she had to be the best at everything. For months, he had been trying to find the right set of circumstances, which would allow him to seek his revenge on the appalling Petronella, but so far, nothing had come to mind.

Then Big Wart arrived at school.

Without thinking, as the last table tumbled to the floor and the cruel punishment was dished out, Mercury meticulously cast his spell. As soon as he had finished, Petronella's teeth fell out and grass began to grow!

And boy did it grow.

Panicking, she held her mouth so the strands of green wouldn't show and ran to the girls' loo. Aghast and in horror, she looked at the grass growing out of her mouth from the gaps where her front teeth had been.

Chapter 6

This was the end for Petronella; how could she hope to impress Big Wart with grass growing from her mouth? Thankfully, her quota of kissing in the lower school was over until September.

She sat on down on one of the benches and thought, how had this happened? The obvious thing was to go to the reference part of the library, and find out about grass-growing-gums. Whilst locked up in a cubicle in the girls' loo, she also thought about finding a help group, to see if there was anybody else in the world with this problem.

It wasn't life-threatening at this stage, but if it was a joke she was sure as anything: she was going to sort out the perpetrator.

Once   everyone   had   left   school,

she gathered up her grass,

wound it into a ball,

tied it with an elastic band,

and tried to hide it down

the inside of her coat.

Worse,
Petronella
went home crying
(something the
Pumpernickel-Pinkstocking-Bercks
never did).

Chapter 7

'See! I told ya if ya messed around with boys with black'eads an' warts, somethin' would 'appen.

Loo' at all tha' grass where ya front teeth shoul' be! Didn' I say somethin' would 'appen?

Didn' I tell ya? Now look at tha' stupid grass growing in yer front gums! You look as if you should be grazin'!'

Her mother shouted at her as she cut the morning grass in Petronella's mouth, which was shooting like mad since the sun had been shining.

Worse than that, her mother was now favouring her younger step-whatever who had been left in a commercial-sized washing-powder box on the door-step of their house as a baby.

Suddenly, Catronella was the favourite. Could this be because Ma couldn't get to grips with the grass growing in her daughter's mouth, or, did she  *really* have enough love for two children? She wasn't quite sure, but all Petronella knew was that she didn't like grass – especially in her mouth – and, was this a curse? If so, how would she get her old teeth back? And what about Big Wart; how could she sort this out?

'I knew sumthin' real bad was gonna 'appen. Kissin' an' warts don't mix!

You should've got on with them studies for this bi' of English, heaven knows when you'll need to write a tractor form for a livin'!' stormed her mother as she whipped up a couple of tyres for a spare broken-down truck in the yard.

'As if the day's no' busy enough with gettin' the tractors and stuff sorted out for town, I've got to think of this now. Put tha' grass away, it's dribbling' everywhere!! And another thing, how ya gonna eat yer broth an' beans? Are ya gonna cut yer grass before or after yer eat?'

Ma Metronella really wasn't having much sympathy with her daughter's plight, and the unusual tears didn't help either. As Petronella cut the new grass in her mouth, she wondered if this was a form of food poisoning; perhaps it was the result of school lunch – she didn't know. All she could think about was her delight at reaching her kissing quota so early in the summer term.

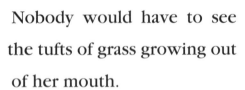

Nobody would have to see the tufts of grass growing out of her mouth.

Chapter 8

That night, she tied the long strands behind the nape of her neck before she ate, and plaited it before she went to sleep, in the hopes of it falling off and out.

This new situation meant she wouldn't be able to have her beguiling power over boys, and they would stop being obedient.

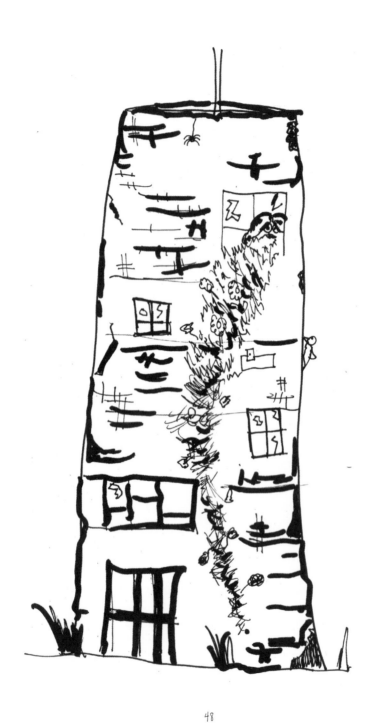

When she awoke next morning, the grass had reached the hall of the **third floor**, and this was a worry because her bedroom was on the **fifth floor**.

As she heaved herself out of bed, Petronella screamed in disbelief; it was like a carpet starting from her gums.

After cutting off the morning grass, she slunk down to breakfast where her father greeted her,

'So Petrol, I gather we've got a **little extra** grass growin' around the place. Hmmm. Hmmm. Now Petrol, my pet, don' let this little bi' of grass upset ya, I can always feed the cows or let ma lovely pigs roll abou' in the yard with it... don' ya worry.' and he patted her on the head whilst gathering up the grass.

'I can't go to school like this!! Everybody will think I'm a freak!' Poor old Petronella bawled her eyes out, which was now quite a complicated matter. The tears got lost in the grass, and for some reason, blowing your nose had its problems as well.

'Loo' just ge' yerself off to school and cut the grass 'tween lessons. I'll send a note into ya form tutor. Oh, an' make sure ya don't get any birds stuck in that grass in break or lunch!' bawled her heartless and cruel mother. Petronella and Catronella – or 'The-Vacuum-with-a-Face' (as

she was nick–named), got ready to tractor off to school.

'Never mind Petrol,'

boomed her father, 'them boys should love you for the person ya are, even if ya look a bit like a haystack. Don' ya take any rubbish from anyone or I'll take ma shot-gun down in ma new tractor!' Pa was always

so good like that. Catronella smiled, didn't talk, just smirked and wiped her white high heels before mounting her own tractor to drive to school.

Chapter 9

Petronella sniffled, and cried with rage, at the thought of all those wimp-like boys sniggering and laughing at her.

As she rode through the town on her tractor, ignoring the traffic lights on red, Petronella had a brainwave; she could, and would, turn this experience to her advantage!

On reaching the school gates, she stood tall on her tractor. Waving her arms like a

warrior ready for war, her uniform was brandished like armour-plating awaiting its battle.

She was the **Angel** of **Boudicca** sent on a quest to fight serpents, crocodiles, the odd dragon, and to save all majorettes from snapped canes! Her blazer was now a cloak, her satchel no longer was a haven for books, rather tomes of wisdom and spells. From now on, her only homework would be to perfect her dealings with the **Gods of Boudicca!**

Chapter 10

By **eight forty-three precisely**, Petronella had an army of followers who had signed up to conquer any potential crocodiles or dragons, and were scavenging the school corridors and playgrounds.

By **eight-fifty**, teachers had been ushered back into the staffroom, whilst the new heroine, along with her army, checked the grounds for any danger.

By **nine o'clock**, it had been decided that the school was safe as long as her magic and mystical grass walked the halls of power.

By **nine-fifteen**, it had been decided that, until further notice, Petronella Pumpernickel-Pinkstocking-Berck was relieved from the duty of school and work. Her mission demanded far greater and admiral feats – to prepare for battle.

In the staffroom, teachers were given emergency talks on avoiding a nuclear war, and each had a gas mask in case things got messy. Indeed, they all decided, even if they died, this was far better than doing work and marking books. Some even wondered if these would be their last days on earth. If so, they would watch Star Wars in lessons, to prepare for a possible invasion. Of course, there were some of the teaching staff who wanted to be with their loved ones. So they sniffled over digestive biscuits as they snivelled over family memories, and knelt on the staffroom floor.

Petronella stormed the corridors rather loving the new look; all this for Big Wart. He'd better notice or else she'd have to give him to her army to sort out.

The rest of the student population suddenly bowed, or whispered her name quietly as she strode by. Her boots, clicked on the floors, and the buttons on her blazer swiped black-headed urchins and pupils in her way, as she patrolled the school.

Chapter 11

It was going better than she had expected. She flexed the saucepan-cum-balloon shaped muscles in her arms. By nine-thirty the male population was sparring over who would be the next in line for a "Pumpernickel Holdfast". Each spotty, weak, wimpy male, hoped secretly that it would be him.

Catronella had been made, on the spur-of-the-moment, chief designer for her tufts at grass-roots. **Big Wart was to be her general**, if **only** he would leave the pink tunics and white petal shoes alone. Some of her other friends would be slaves. As for the rest of the army; they would just be on call.

Petronella thought she ought to have a vision and decided to copy bits from Halloween films.

She suddenly screamed,

waved her massive balloon-like arms in the air and started shouting. It was a mixture of French, German and Liverpool, with a bit of bad language stuck in the middle, as she didn't want to abuse her new status.

Ah, Petronella thought, there was a lot to bless for this green grass; perhaps it would start a fashion trend. Big Wart had to notice her now – grass or no grass, she was a force to be noticed.

Giving positions of authority to those closest or 'best friends' is never a wise move.

This became perfectly clear, when instead of designing ways to present the increasingly long grass, Catronella was more concerned about choosing colour-coordinated armour which would match her hair and eyes. So she was still on the internet when called to conference.

Big Wart, although he had massive shoulders, actually had a very small brain, which seemed at the moment, to settle only on anything associated with majorettes. So he was also late for his first general's conference.

Chapter 12

In fact, Big Wart didn't know there was a war, or that the school was on high security. Although, he did think the tufts of grass were quite cool for a bruiser like Petronella.

'Er Petronella, cor this is a big name for me, I don' do big names. Can I call ya Pet?'

he asked as he perched on the side of a table reading his football scores to his waiting fans. They giggled, Catronella smiled; he was dim but she liked him - even with spots and warts he was sort of cute.

From the front of the class, Petronella stood tall and firm, her head high, the blazer like a symbol of protection. She neatly and calmly parted her grass and yelled,

 'Nobody **EVER EVER** calls me PET!!'

Then, just as she was about to explode into a tirade, she caught his eyes looking serious.

Calming down she replied,

'Well, just this once. Actually, Pa calls me Petrol…'

Big Wart gave a disgusted grunt, looked away, and flicked through his comic.

'Petrol is for bikes an' cars, not for a sweet, gentle female like you.' sniggered Big Wart who was quite enjoying all this war stuff. School, he decided, wasn't bad at all; not many could say they had an Angel of Boudicca in their midst.

Chapter 13

Realising that Big Wart wasn't going to take the invasion or war seriously, Petronella changed tactics, 'Wart-Face, I don't think you're up to being a general, so I'm giving the job to someone else. You don't mind do you?' she asked, tweaking her tufts of grass. She smirked as she saw him gasp in horror at the thought of his new fan club, 'The Mini Dimples', no longer having a leader or a role model.

'Aw, c'mon Petronella, it was jus' a joke...' he spluttered, as he thought what else he could put on his CV for a job. It was certain he'd never get any GCSEs, except for majorettes or something like that. Uh, he'd have to think of something else. His river-sized chest wasn't going to get him out of this; war wasn't going to be easy with her in charge.

'Fing is Petrol, I have to go now as I have a rehearsal for...' he whispered it, as if he had committed a crime, 'majorettes. I'm sort of the mascot.'

The class stood open-mouthed whilst the Angel of Boudicca glowered, and clipped her green tufts whilst flexing her saucepan-style arms.

'Well, we'll send you a pink pair of ballet shoes or white tights to help you along...'

The novelty of the big muscles, his shoulders, the combed wrist hair, had worn off. She looked closely at his skin; far too many blackheads for her liking. 'Well, you better go to the majorettes, after all they are so important.' And she continued to talk to the rest of her troops who were all consumed by every word she said.

Chapter 14

It wasn't until much later when the army was disturbed by the sound of wailing and crying down the corridor.

At first they thought **aliens had invaded**.

Then they thought it was **ghosts of warriors past**. How amazed they were when they saw their huge general crumpled on the corridor floor up against a wall, nursing his feet.

Wearing the high heels had really hurt them; his feet were bleeding badly. Big Wart, after being hit accidentally by the majorettes with their canes, had decided war was a much safer option, but wondered if his esteemed Boudicca would accept him back as her general.

Hobbling into the classroom, he announced his retirement from the show-business world of majorettes, saying he was worthy of more than being a mascot. 'Fing is Petrol, I know I shouldn't have left the team an' all that stuff, but I didn't know my calling was to follow the signal of war...'

'Hang on!' snapped the Angel of Boudicca, flouncing round the classroom with her grass between her feet and in her shoes. 'You **were a mascot** so now you want to fight a **war** until your feet get better? Give us a break!!'

Meanwhile, everyone at school worried about what would happen, and if Petronella could save them from crocodiles or even dragons.

For the rest of the week, the school stayed under the watchful eyes of the Angel of

Boudicca and her fearsome army, who had not seen anything strange.

The staff meekly went on their way, waiting for something terrible to occur, so ate a continuous supply of digestive biscuits. Everyone was waiting for something to happen, something

big, bad and **r a t h e r terrible.**

Chapter 15

Something bad did happen to Petronella each day. When she awoke, not only did her grass continue to grow from her gums at a rate of knots, but the day also brought new visions, generally taken from clippings of horror and Halloween movies. These were mixed into the school day as part of the war on aliens and such-like.

The grass continued to grow. Her breath smelt of a sweet manure, and the grass was no longer brushed with a comb; it was now tended to by a rake with a shortened handle. Added to this, lots of small, creepy creatures had made nests in her green mane.

Catronella really liked her new role of designing the bird-ridden tufts of grass into strange shapes. She was often seen reading hairstyle magazines down the corridor, as she trailed the ever-growing grass, which actually weighed quite a lot.

She felt immensely important and smiled all the time. Her conversation was limited to monosyllabic replies, with a glittering smile and a giggle, which she did 'terribly' well.

She loved not having to do the same things as all the other students. **She loved** it even more, when she was asked about the Angel's visions. **She just loved** herself, and insisted on a new tractor for school. Of course, this new fame demanded much more from the delicious Catronella. So, she asked for her very

own Sentence Completer – which **everybody** in positions of authority had.

Ma Metronella P u m p e r n i c k e l - Pinkstocking-Berck sold her most lavish pig-trussling tractors, for the most beautiful, and almost monosyllabic Catronella, who now refused to complete the most simple of sentences.

Petronella was horrified at her parents' desire to keep the 'Vacuum-with-a-Face' happy. She was the important one.

She was sure the Angel of Boudicca needed the Sentence Completer, far more than the white-high-heeled 'Vacuum-with-a-Face'!

'Ma it's not fair!! Wha' about me? I am the Angel of Boudicca an' I don' get anything, not even a shampoo for my grass!!

It's not fair!'

Chapter 16

Petronella stormed and rampaged out of the industrial-looking house, kicking the poor helpless pigs, geese and cows in her path.

As she stamped through the yard trailing grass from her mouth, Pa looked on fondly, watching his little green haystack throwing a tractor or two in rage. Nothing beat his little Petrol to light up the darkness in his life. She was his beauty, his adorable, sweet, emotional girl, he had a soft spot for her – and the grass did come in handy for them pigs and cows as well.

'Now, ya listen Petronella, she ain't the same as you, our little Catronella. First of all, she smel' so swee' in tha' big box of washin' powder back when we found her. She neverrr says owt wrong! She's just sweet, an' look how she's made tha' grass look good each day. There's never a blade out of place. Besides, she don't ask for much, does she Ma?' Ma smiled at her husband of five hundred and twenty years and nodded at him. The furious angel grabbed her tonnes of tuft and disappeared.

On top of everything, the war, this dangerous mystical war, wasn't going well at school. She couldn't fit into the lift with her grass as there was so much.

This meant that her slaves had to carry it all the time; she was far too important to do such things, besides, she had to occupy her adoring fans.

She also needed to have a rebellion in school. Everyone had become too accepting of the high security alert. The teachers were now happy about marking – they were even grateful, as they hadn't been savaged in a nuclear war.

Big Wart, terrified of being asked to wear high heels and a tunic that squeezed his chest, and made it hurt, had started to sound just a bit on the intelligent side. Though, the great thing was, because Mercury Bitterack's spell was still working, Petronella didn't do school work or attend lessons. Secretly, she was worried and had now started to pray at night that the grass would stay.

She had already missed class for nearly five weeks, and not a crocodile or dragon, in sight.

Chapter 17

After a while everything became normal. Catronella got bored of her Sentence Completer, as he kept on putting words into her mouth. Ma went back to throwing her tractors at annoying situations. The staff had meetings, and the students began to enjoy their clubs. Big Wart decided to give the majorettes another go. Pa kept adding more bits of metal to the house, and Mercury continued to be angry at Petronella.

Life was normal in an abnormal sort of way. The Angel of Boudicca decided she had to have a revolt, but she was unsure how and where.

And the grass continued to grow. It grew so much that her jaw ached. Even when she cut it, the stuff returned to fill her mouth, which made talking difficult at times.

Of course, Mercury Bitterack was delighted. Petronella's fame had subsided, making it perfectly normal for students to see a trail of grass everywhere. Her army slowly dispersed over time, as other things took priority in school, such as plays and sports days.

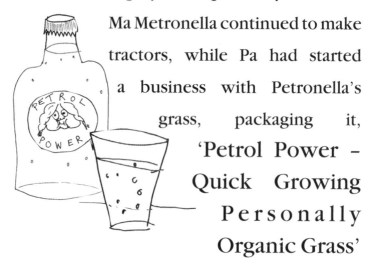

Ma Metronella continued to make tractors, while Pa had started a business with Petronella's grass, packaging it, 'Petrol Power – Quick Growing Personally Organic Grass' designed to be used in juices for energy.

And, it seemed, that after the horror and danger surrounding the Angel of Boudicca, everything else was unimportant. Life was just normal - well except for the grass growing in Petronella's

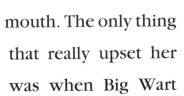

mouth. The only thing that really upset her was when Big Wart asked Catronella out on a date, to watch a Majorettes competition. Petronella fumed, until Pa pointed out one or two things.

'Now my little Petrol, don' you

worry about that date.
Remember, tha'
Wart boy - he
can' read can he?
Well no' much. An'
Catronella, now don'
get me wrong, I love her, even though she
were found in a washing-powder box - or
summit like tha'. Well, our little Catronella,
she just don' finish her sentences, so you never
quite know wha' she might be meaning. So,

my little Petrol, with all the
fame of the grass an' all, an'
readin' and finishin'
sentences - you
might be a little
bored', he
said gently as
he cut a new stack

of grass for his juice business. This was now becoming quite famous and making the family rich.

Petronella, as part of his publicity campaign, was photographed in magazines, her grass beautifully combed and examples of the juice alongside her Angel of Boudicca pose. As her new fame grew, so did her new fan club and there was curiosity over the grass sprouting from her mouth. In fact, she had a small group of fans who

were trying to stick grass seeds into their gums to grow grass in the same way.

Deep down, Petronella was **fed up** of the grass; she found it difficult to talk and eat properly and worried if she'd stay like this forever. She also worried whether she'd still have the grass when she was old and, more importantly, if it would turn grey.

But **even worse than that**, she had to have a battle to show her power.

She needed to regain control of the school, so that she wouldn't have to go to lessons or do homework. And, she needed to get Big Wart's admiration back.

Chapter 18

Just as she thought everything was lost and nothing was worthwhile, **something happened**.

One night as she was combing her grass, the phone rang; it was school.

A **dragon** was invading the premises and both the old, doddery caretakers couldn't deal with the flames, so could Petronella come and sort the monster out? Frozen in horror at the thought of slaying a **'real' dragon,** she wondered how big it was, and if it really had **flames** spouting out of its mouth, or if it could fly – just like all the ones she'd read about in school. In a kind of fear and excitement, Petronella found herself saying to the caretakers that she was on her way! Grabbing her father from his workshop, where he was hammering new bits of scrap to the house, they flew to school on Ma Metronella's new hi-tec tractor, which could fly, if the wind was in the right direction.

At the school gates, teachers were gathered, crying in fear at the thought of the school going up in flames: whilst hordes of pupils were praying it would do just that. The school seemed to be divided into two sides: those wishing to save the school, and those hoping the dragon was real, and would blow-torch it down with his flames.

It was a difficult decision for Petronella to make.

She didn't know whether she should keep the pupils or the staff happy. The main thing in her mind was to appear strong, a bit like the real Queen Boudicca.

The wings of the dragon spanned the width of classrooms, and as it swooped down, it blew its flames at everything in its path. Smoke and fumes choked the onlookers, who were now all getting a little tired of the fire. Everyone looked towards Petronella and her father, as they strode towards the monster, who seemed to be smiling, as flames spat out of his mouth towards the public.

'It's OK folks, we'll give it our best shot to sort this dragon out!' Trying to sound sure of her future actions, she strode towards its enormous face, and stared into the bulging, green and black eyes, which seemed to be laughing at the whole situation.

Chapter 19

The dragon sat perched on top of the roof, with his long neck and scaly face, bending down the wall of the dining hall, puffing gently as it rested. Every now and then, as it yawned, flames slithered from its mouth which revealed **very large, grey and black teeth.** Yawning, he breathed out. Petronella gasped.

'You've go' bad breath. When was the las' time you brushed ya teeth?' she shouted to the bulging eyes and scaly skin, which dripped slime. The dragon looked closely into her eyes, stared at her, and bared his teeth.

She saw this enormous cave-like hole, with a tongue and teeth – long, grey, black teeth which curled to a point. Then, she noticed a huge, swollen lump over one of the teeth at the back, which was dripping with blood.

'When was the las' time ya saw a dentist?' she shouted to him as he roared.

The dragon just stopped still. He was puzzled. Wasn't she meant to be frightened? He'd been taught at dragon school that humans were always terrified of dragons. But this one seemed different. He'd never seen a human with grass coming out of its mouth in *any* of the text books at school. He then let out an enormous whimper which blew out some flames.

The crowd, police, army, and of course, Big Wart, gasped at her bravery, standing so near the dragon and not being scared. Petronella smiled. She could use this to her advantage and be seen as a heroine once again. The crowd held their breath as she asked the dragon to lower his head, and open his mouth. The crowd was silent as the dragon relaxed. He  opened his mouth, and rested his head on the side of the school roof. Parting her long grass from her mouth, she asked to be raised up by his tail.

The dragon drew up his tail with Petronella on it, towards his mouth.

'Yer breath stinks! Open wide!' she shouted. Holding her nose she peered into this huge, horrible hole and with her sword touched the swelling on the back tooth.

The dragon yelped out loud and the crowd were sure they saw tears. In the gum, at the back, was a piece of wood stuck near a tooth. It was sore.

This was the root of all the trouble. So, pulling out her sword, Petronella, dug out the long spike of wood which was causing the pain. Then she cut some grass and bathed the sore wound with it.

Chapter 20

A gentle **purring** sound came from the dragon as he smiled and wagged his tail. The **crowd, police, special forces** and, of course, **national television,** all **shouted** and **cheered**.

Petronella stroked the dragon's face and wiped away any tears with more of her grass.

Then, she sat by his head whilst stroking him to sleep.

The crowd still stood and waited.

Nobody moved for hours until the dragon awoke. Instead of raising his head to blow flames, with his tail he lifted Petronella onto

his back and flew into the sky. As they soared into the sky, the world watched, and was **amazed**.

They were not amazed at the dragon, its pain, or Petronella flying on its back; they were amazed that all the grass from her mouth had disappeared.

Of course, so was Mercury Bitterack, who had forgotten that the spell would be lifted from Petronella, if she ever rode on the back of a dragon.

So, by the time they landed, Petronella was the most famous and brave girl in the whole world, and everyone wanted to see the dragon, who was now devoted to her. This attention meant that she was **far too important** to notice Big Wart – there were far more exciting boys who liked dragons.

As for Ma and Pa, they made the house where Petronella had grown her grass, into a museum of bravery and success.

In the meantime, Catronella felt she had to do something worthwhile,

so finished a sentence completing course and passed her tractor-driving test.

Big Wart, realising how foolish he'd been, sent presents to Petronella's house every day:

new tractors,
steam rollers,
the odd combine harvester...

But it was no good, nothing worked.

It was all too late.

Petronella was having far too much fun with her own personal dragon, and was on top of the world. She didn't ride a tractor to school any more.

No, she went to school by dragon – as you do!!

Biography

Anne Stairmand was born in North Yorkshire, living much of her life in villages near the Cleveland Hills. After graduating, she worked in education, teaching in both primary and secondary schools in the south east, working in the advisory service and as part of a leadership team.

Dividing her time, she now writes books for children and adults, and has her own business as a bespoke jeweller, with her own hallmark and stamp, specialising in silver, pearls and commissions. She is married with a grown-up family and lives on the Suffolk Essex border.

Become an author for a day!

Anne is available for author visits to schools which are stimulating. Using her expertise in literacy and education, she supplies a package that is not only challenging and innovative but can help improve writing back in the classroom.

Resources linked to the curriculum are made to cater for each class/group, so afterwards can be used as a tool to support literacy at KS1, KS2 and KS3.

Fun days with lots of excitement which also develop writing and literacy skills.

A variety of packages available to suit needs, enjoyment and, of course, budget.

Contact:
Email: annestairmandj@hotmail.co.uk
www.annestairmand.co.uk